DEADLINE

by Simon Cheshire

First published 2011 by
A & C Black Publishers Ltd
36 Soho Square, London, W1D 3QY

www.acblack.com

ISBN: 978-1-4081-3110-7

A CIP catalogue for this book is available from the British Library.

This book is produced using paper that is made from wood grown in
managed, sustainable forests. It is natural, renewable and recyclable.
The logging and manufacturing processes conform to the
environmental regulations of the country of origin.

Printed and bound in Great Britain
by CPI Cox & Wyman, Reading RG1 8EX.

DEADLINE

Simon Cheshire

A & C Black • London

CONTENTS

CHAPTER ONE

ARREST

It was just gone six in the morning when the back door of Sam's house was kicked in.

He was half awake, half asleep, his hand drifting lazily over the Snooze button on his alarm clock. Eleven-year-old Sam would often swim up from the depths of sleep a few minutes before the clock started bleating, and then snake one arm out from under the warmth of the bedclothes to turn it off. He didn't want to hear that blasted thing today. It was half term. He didn't want to think about school at all, or about how he'd be leaving Year 6 at the end of term, or worry about starting at a whole new school –

BANG!

His eyes flicked open. What on earth was...?

BANG!

He heard wood splintering. Then a third crash from downstairs.

Sam quickly propped himself up on one elbow,

rubbing sleep from his eyes. Had Mum dropped a tray or something?

Daylight glowed in a soft fringe around the curtains. The familiar, neatly tidy shapes of his room were visible as outlines in the semi-darkness. For a second or so, there was silence.

Suddenly, a scream sliced through the house. Sam flinched with fright.

He flung the sheets aside, and leapt out into the cooler air of the room. He fumbled with the door handle.

On the landing, his twelve-year-old sister Karen was peering blearily out from behind her door, her face surrounded by a halo of scraggy blonde hair. "Whassat noise?" she cried. "Whozat?"

Sam was too scared to answer. The sudden way he'd woken up and jumped out of bed had left him wondering if this was real.

He knew he wasn't dreaming when he heard a second scream. This one was followed by more bumps and crashes from downstairs, and the sounds of other voices. Loud ones, yelling commands.

Sam hesitated. Mum was in trouble and he had to… but… who were these people? Burglars? Armed robbers? A thousand thoughts tore through his head, half of them shouting at him to do something, half of them shouting at him to run away, fast.

Footsteps padded quickly behind him. Karen, flinging her dressing gown around herself, dashed past him and ran down the stairs, her bare feet thudding against the steps.

Sam followed her, his heart galloping. As they reached the hallway below, they could see that the door to the kitchen was flung open so far it creaked back on its hinges.

A blast of chill early morning air hit them. Sam could see that the back door, leading out into the garden, had been forced open and was leaning at a disjointed angle.

But it was the figure standing in the kitchen doorway who got their attention. The man was almost as broad as he was tall, and for a second or so he didn't notice them. Then his dark eyes, glaring out from underneath a large cap, locked onto them.

"Two more here!" he cried.

He was a police officer. A walkie-talkie was clipped to his chest, and a black F-shaped riot stick swung from his belt.

"You! You!" he yelled, stabbing a finger at each of them. "Get in there! Now!"

He booted the living room door open. As he

strode forward, a second policeman appeared behind him. This one was dragging Mum by the collar of her shirt.

"Mum!" cried Sam and Karen in unison.

Before she could answer, Mum was violently pulled into the hallway. Then she was shoved into the living room and out of sight.

"Shut up!" the first cop shouted at Sam and Karen. "Get in there too! Move!"

He snatched them by their shoulders and

pushed them ahead of him. They fell in a heap beside the bookshelves that ran along one end of the living room.

Sam twisted around and sat in a ball, his back pressed up against the radiator. Three more cops were looming in front of the window, silhouetted against the daylight filtering in through the net curtains. These three were all carrying guns.

Images flashed across Sam's mind: from all the adventure stories he'd read, all the action movies he'd seen. A thousand times, he'd wished real life was more like books and films. Right now, however, with guns and police in his living room, he wasn't so sure.

One of the armed cops, a thin, pale man with a scar that crossed his lips like an exclamation mark, snapped back the hammer of his handgun and aimed it at Sam.

"You know why we're here," he said calmly to Mum. "How do you connect?"

"Leave the kids alone!" screamed Mum. "They aren't involved! They know nothing about this!"

The thin cop smiled grimly. "I don't doubt that for a moment." He leaned forward and pressed the barrel of the gun against Sam's head. "Now, how...do you...connect?"

"Under the stairs," hissed Mum. She glanced over at Sam and Karen. They couldn't interpret the strange look on her face. It was one they'd never seen before.

The thin cop nodded at the tall one who'd dragged Mum out of the kitchen. The tall one went out into the hall and flung open the door to the large understairs storage area. This was Mum's home office.

Wedging himself into the small swivel chair inside, he switched on Mum's computer, slotted a thumb drive into one of the USB ports, and scanned through the data that scrolled across the screen.

He put the USB drive back in his pocket, stood up, and kicked the computer to pieces. A dozen or more violent blows reduced it to splinters of plastic and circuit board. He returned to the living room.

"Upload was set to nine o'clock," he grunted. "Looks like we caught it in time."

The thin cop smiled at Mum. The scar across his lip creased horribly. "Lucky you," he whispered. He stepped back from Sam and turned his gun on Mum. "Now get up. You're coming with us."

Mum and Karen both started shouting at once,

a series of 'no's and 'why's and 'what for's. The thin cop pushed Sam and Karen onto the sofa.

"You two might know nothing," he said quietly, "but Mummy knows plenty. And we'd like her to tell us all about it. And if you two start making a fuss, or telling your friends we were here, or talking to your teachers about this, then Mummy won't be coming home. Ever. Got that?"

Sam and Karen glared up at him. Sam felt he ought to have something to say, something witty or cleverly sarcastic. But his mind was blank, wiped clear by fright.

"Take her out," said the thin cop. The tall one grabbed Mum again and marched her ahead of him, holding her arms in painful V-shapes behind her back.

"Hey, boss, should we tell her she's under arrest?"

"If you like," chuckled the thin cop.

All five police officers moved into the hall, then out on to the street. One or two of the neighbours were at their windows, or putting out the bins, watching what was going on.

Mum twisted around and called to the children. "I was meeting Mr Collins...about the wedding dress. Tell him I'm busy at work."

She was bundled into one of two waiting

police cars. The five officers piled in too. None of them so much as glanced back at the house. The two cars revved up and accelerated away, their exhausts belching.

Sam and Karen stood by the open front door, staring, dazed, hardly believing what was happening.

"Why? I don't…" began Sam.

"What's Mum done?" breathed Karen. "What's she done wrong?"

"… Who the heck is Mr Collins?" said Sam.

CHAPTER TWO

MR COLLINS

Sam and Karen sat on the sofa in the living room. The place was eerily quiet now. Silent and empty. No sounds of Mum getting breakfast ready. No sound at all. No Mum.

They sat in silence, their minds buzzing with what they'd just witnessed. Sam was trying not to panic. He'd never been the sort to stay calm in a crisis. Karen scratched at her still-uncombed hair with both hands.

"Let's think about this," she said, mostly to herself. "We'll get dressed, we'll go down to the police station, there'll be someone there who'll help us."

Sam's urge to start running up and down and screaming was getting stronger by the minute. "Something's not right," he muttered.

"You think?" said Karen. "Mum's been dragged off by the cops, yeah, hmm, what's wrong with this picture?"

"I mean something's not right about those cops," said Sam. "I've read loads of crime stories, and I've seen loads of cop shows, and I'm telling you there was something very odd about those police officers."

Karen looked puzzled. Her hands paused in mid-scratch. "Like what?"

"Well," said Sam, taking a deep breath. He was trying to steady his nerves and stop himself shaking with fright, but his voice was still fluttering like tissue paper in a hurricane. "I know that books and movies and things like that get a lot of stuff wrong about how the police really do things, but they do try to get the basics right."

"Yes, so?"

"So when have you ever seen a police officer point a gun at a kid?" said Sam. "Or threaten to shoot someone if someone else doesn't spill the beans? Or smash up computers? Or throw people around who aren't being violent?"

Karen thought for a moment. "But they do kick doors in. And they do drag people away."

"Not like that," protested Sam. "Remember what they said? I'm sure they're supposed to arrest people properly, you know, with all that 'I'm arresting you on suspicion of...' and so on. There are rules. There are regulations. If cops don't stick

16

to the rules they get into big trouble."

"If they haven't got Chief Inspector Whatever standing over them watching, I don't suppose they care," said Karen.

"It doesn't work like that," said Sam. "Look at us. They've left us here. On our own. They've taken Mum off somewhere, not said where, and they've left us here alone. I'm in Year 6, you're in Year 7, it's the middle of half term and they've just left us here. Isn't that illegal, or something?"

For several minutes, there was silence. Karen smoothed her hair absent-mindedly, but it just sprang back into its usual bird's nest. "You know," she said quietly, "I think you might be right."

"What if those men weren't from the police at all?" said Sam. The feeling of panic was about to leak out of his eyes.

"Then who on earth were they? Why disguise themselves like that?" said Karen.

"I think Mum knew who they were," shuddered Sam. "She was scared, but she didn't seem very surprised. Did you notice?"

Karen nodded slowly. "That might explain the weird thing she said. About this Mr Collins and the wedding dress. Perhaps she was trying to tell us something?"

"Well, I wish she'd told it a bit clearer," said

Sam. "What are we supposed to make of it? Who's Mr Collins, for goodness' sake?"

"Oh, use your brain," grumbled Karen. "If it was a message for us, she must have thought we'd be able to understand it. She must be referring to something specific."

They crept out into the hallway. Mum's address book was lying amongst the stuff that had been knocked off her understairs desk. No Mr Collins, Mrs Collins, or any other sort of Collins.

"Could it be an anagram?" said Sam.

"Of what?" snorted Karen. "O'Slincl? Socnill? Lolscin?"

"Alright, alright," muttered Sam. He went back into the living room. What would a detective in one of his favourite books do? Not let his insides turn runny, that was for sure!

Think! Think! Mum must have made that message up on the spot. You wouldn't go around with hidden messages for your kids at the ready, just in case you were dragged away first thing in the morning! Would you? No, definitely not.

"So," muttered Sam to himself, "if Mum thought up that message, and knew we'd work it out, it must be based on something right here, something right in front of us."

He stood staring at the bookcase for at least

five minutes before it finally occurred to him: the books, a huge collection of words, the perfect place to hide a message!

Mr Collins about the wedding dress.

Sam glanced along the spines of the books, his head cocked to one side. He couldn't see anything with a wedding in the title. After a few minutes, he spotted:

The Woman in White by Wilkie Collins.

He almost gasped. Mr Collins. A woman in white. A wedding dress.

"Got it!" cried Sam. He quickly slid the book out of its place on the shelf. Karen was at his shoulder.

"I don't get it," said Karen. "What does it mean? Surely we've not got to read that whole book to work it out. It's enormous."

Sam opened the book and flicked through it. It fell open about halfway through. A small, rectangular section had been hollowed out in the centre of about thirty pages.

Sitting inside the hollow was a standard SD card, the same sort of data card Sam used in his camera.

"Mum's a web designer," muttered Karen. "What data could she possibly need to keep hidden like this? If she wants to stop someone

finding something, all she's got to do is leave it in the mess on her desk!"

"One thing's for sure," said Sam. "We have got to take a look at what's on this card."

CHAPTER THREE

INTERCEPT

Deeeeng-doooooong!

The doorbell made them both jump. They shot nervous glances at each other. Should they answer it? They weren't expecting anyone. Could those 'police' have come back?

"I don't think they'd ring the bell, do you?" said Karen.

She went to the door. It was Mrs Willis from down the road. The old woman blinked at Karen from behind a pair of glasses which were way too big for her face.

"Hello, Karen, love, is everything alright?" she said quietly. A tissue was scrunched up in her bony hand. "Only, umm, I heard a bit of a noise."

"Oh, yes, everything's fine, Mrs Willis," said Karen hurriedly. "No problem."

"Only, umm, I heard shouting," mouthed Mrs Willis. "And as you three are on your own, I wondered if everything was alright."

"We're totally OK, really, thanks," said Karen, doing her best to smile. Behind her, listening, Sam wondered for a moment why she didn't yell, "We're in danger! Help! Get the cops!" right in Mrs Willis's face. But all the questions which were spinning around his head soon suggested to him that whatever Mum was mixed up in might be made even worse if outside help got involved.

"Only, umm, I couldn't help noticing the police were here," whispered Mrs Willis, leaning towards Karen as if Karen might not have realised that already. "I couldn't help noticing that, umm, they dragged your mum away."

"Ah, yeah," muttered Karen. "She'd forgotten to pay a parking ticket. They're really hot on that around here."

Mrs Willis went slightly pale. She scrunched the tissue tighter. "Oh, I see. Well, as long as everything's alright."

"Oh, it's fine, thanks."

A couple of minutes later, Mrs Willis was back at home making sure Mr Willis hadn't got any unpaid parking fines. Meanwhile, Sam had fetched Karen's laptop from her room.

He blew the dust off it. "I thought you were supposed to use this for your homework," he said.

Karen shrugged. "I can never be bothered."

Sam booted up the machine and slotted the SD card into its reader.

The laptop clicked and ticked a little as it opened the card's contents and set them out on its desktop.

"Wow, there's tonnes of stuff here," muttered Sam.

The computer's desktop displayed a long, scrolling parade of labelled icons. The majority showed up as blank-looking rectangles, files which the operating system couldn't identify as belonging to a particular programme or file type.

"I expect there was a lot of specialised software on Mum's computer," said Karen. "Web authoring kit."

"Yes, that makes sense," said Sam. "But if that's true, a lot of these files have got very odd names. Look, they're strings of letters, like they're encoded, or something."

"I'm sure Mum does plenty of web design work which is confidential," said Karen. "Stuff that's for companies who won't want their website ideas leaked to competitors, that sort of thing."

"Yeah, but would you really need to turn it all into funny-looking code?" said Sam. "What's wrong with just password-protecting your hard drive?"

"Never heard of industrial espionage?" said Karen. "It's not just governments who spy on each other, you know."

Sam got a strange, icy feeling in his head. "Do you think that's what this is all about?" he whispered. "Do you think those men were working for the rivals of one of Mum's customers?"

Karen glanced at him nervously. "I don't know what to think. Keep looking. There must be something important on this card, something that we're meant to find. Otherwise Mum wouldn't have led us to it."

Sam worked his way through the listing. He opened a number of files at random. Some of them were nothing more than solid blocks of gibberish. Others were strangely dull documents discussing immensely boring subjects such as aircraft parts, road signs in Eastern European countries, or the addresses of every branch of a high street chain store.

"Weird," said Sam, wrinkling up his nose in mock disgust. "There's nothing that relates to web design here at all."

Karen stared at the computer screen. "Exactly," she mumbled to herself. She reached over and skimmed across the laptop's touchpad, sending the list of files scrolling upwards.

"Go back a bit," she said. "Try some of the other readable ones. Haven't you noticed something?"

Sam grumbled, "You're starting to sound like a teacher."

"I mean it. Go back. There, try those ones!"

Sam did as he was told. More boring office documents written in a style which seemed designed to put anyone reading them to sleep.

"What are you talking about?" said Sam crossly. "What is there to notice?"

"Look at the headers on each document."

Sam got that cold feeling again. Every readable document contained a few lines of reference numbers, printed in much smaller lettering at the top of the first page. Beginning each of those lines was the word "Intercept", followed by a six-digit code, followed by a date.

"Intercept?" he mouthed.

"These are files Mum's got hold of by bugging other computers," breathed Karen. "Look, they're from lots of different places, but they're all marked 'Intercept'. They've been stolen."

"Oh, that's rubbish," groaned Sam. "This is Mum we're talking about, not James Bond."

Slowly, he and his sister turned to look at each other.

Fake cops...guns...hidden data...

"It's not possible," scoffed Sam. "I mean, oh come on! It's... it's impossible!"

Fake cops... guns... hidden data...

His heart was beating like an overheated steam engine. All those books he'd read, all those movies he'd seen. And all the time, working away in her little office under the stairs...

"Impossible!"

Fake cops... guns... hidden data...

His hands pounced on the computer's keyboard.

26

"I've got an idea. If Mum's been intercepting all this stuff for ages, and those men turned up today, then the vital something Mum wants us to find is probably something very recent. Logical, yes?"

"Absolutely," said Karen.

With a series of swift clicks, Sam re-listed the files on the SD card in order of date. The screen blinked. The file at the top was now one labelled 10:42 pm, from the previous evening.

Sam double-clicked on its icon, and it opened. At the top, the usual set of references. Below that, one short paragraph, headed "Text Message from [Suspect Cell B42-43] sent to [Suspect Cell T13-09]". It said:

```
Birthday Card is written and
ready to send.

Party starts 4pm, tomorrow,
Westminster Bridge
```

The only other information contained in the file was a note added below the message:

```
Birthday Card - known code for
high explosive device, as per
intercept 579341
```

For several seconds, Sam and Karen simply gazed at the laptop's screen. Both of them read it several times before the implications of what they'd found sank in.

"This isn't industrial espionage," said Karen. "This is way above that. This afternoon, in London, a bomb's going to go off. And Mum found out about it. And those men who took her must be the bombers. And from what the thug who smashed her computer said, she's the only one who knew. And now, *we're* the only ones who know."

Sam suddenly realised he hadn't taken a breath for several seconds. "Holy...moley," he gasped. "Our mother is a spy."

CHAPTER FOUR

THIRTEEN

As soon as the SD card had been slotted into the laptop, a transmitter inside it had secretly shot a signal out across the internet. The data package re-set and re-sent itself automatically, every few seconds, quietly alerting those who might be watching that the card was active.

From the moment that tiny, hidden transmitter activated, Sam and Karen were in danger.

Miles away from Sam and Karen, in what appeared from the outside to be an abandoned building, a man sat in the shadows between two tall, boarded-up windows. He used an upturned packing crate for a chair, and a fold-out camping table for a desk. His lined and unshaven face was bathed in the glow from a PC screen in front of him. The secrecy of his work meant that those he worked for referred to him only by a number.

This man's number was Two-Twenty-Four.

He'd been awake for almost two days and nights, and he wasn't in the best of moods.

From the far end of the long, cold, shadowy room in which he sat, there came the sound of a door opening and closing. Footsteps approached him through the gloom. A pair of shoes appeared in the thin, dusty shaft of light thrown down through the window boards by the daylight outside.

"You called?" said the visitor. This was his boss, a smartly dressed woman known as Thirteen.

"There's a signal coming from her home address," said Two-Twenty-Four. He hardly bothered to look up from his screen, even though his eyes felt like sandpaper.

"What sort of signal?" said Thirteen.

"I don't think it's anything standard. It's something she's rigged up herself. A basic distress call."

Thirteen grunted angrily. "What set it off?"

"The signal identifies itself as coming from a hidden transmitter inside an SD card used for data backup. Obviously, whoever's activated it doesn't know it's there."

Thirteen let out a long, slow breath. She considered various options. "We have to assume that they've been able to access the data on the card. Which means they may have found out about the Birthday Party plan."

"There's nothing in the signal which will give us access to the computer they're using," said Two-Twenty-Four. "We can't hijack the webcam and ID them."

"Oh, I expect they're using pretty sophisticated kit if they've opened those files. They'll be experts. They'll have thought of that little trick and blocked it."

Thirteen paced back and forth, her heels scratching on the litter of brick dust scattered across the floor. "We don't know who they're working for," she said quietly, "but we do know it isn't us. Which means they must be stopped, right now, before they get in our way. I assume we can home in on the signal?"

Two-Twenty-Four nodded. "No problem. Wherever that SD card goes, we can find it."

"Pack up here. I'll alert the others. We'll send a team after them now," said Thirteen, flipping a phone from her pocket. "Let's hope that card's transmitter stays undetected. With luck, they'll keep it with them, rather than destroy it. That way, they won't have a hope of getting away."

CHAPTER FIVE

TRUST NO ONE

"We're keeping this card safe, with us," said Sam, dropping it into his shirt pocket and buttoning it up. He went back to sorting through the paperwork in Mum's understairs office, feeling slightly more capable now he was dressed. "It's the only lead we've got."

"We're taking it straight to the police, right?" said Karen. "We're not going to let those terrorists push us around and threaten our mum, right?"

Sam pulled sheets of paper out at random, discarding them in a heap next to the shattered remains of Mum's computer. "There's nothing here. It's all about web design, it's just here to back up her cover story. I don't think any of this stuff's been touched in years. She can't have kept anything on paper, or at least nothing connected to her real job."

Karen cleared her throat noisily. "We're taking it straight to the police, right?" she said, louder.

Sam stepped back from the pile of paper and glared at her. "You are joking, aren't you?"

"Of course I'm not joking!" cried Karen. "We are so far out of our depth here, that... that I can't even imagine how far out of our depth we are! We're taking that card, to the cops, now! Or MI5! Or someone!"

"We can't," said Sam. "Think about it. If those guys who turned up here can disguise themselves as police, they could disguise themselves as anyone! They could even have people inside the police. If we go running into the nearest police station blabbering about spies and bombs and stuff, how do we know we won't be walking right into a trap? You see it all the time in spy movies!"

"I suppose you've got a better idea?" scoffed Karen.

"Yes," said Sam. "We go to Westminster Bridge and stop this bomb being planted ourselves! We can't trust anyone. We have no idea who these terrorists are. I for one believe them when they say they'll harm Mum if we tell anyone about all this. It's up to us to take action."

Karen chose her words carefully. "That," she said at last, "wins the gold cup as the single most stupid thing you have ever said. And considering all the many, many stupid things you've said, that's quite an achievement."

"So, what are you going to do, then?" cried Sam. "Sit around in your jim-jams and watch telly all day, like you usually do in the holidays? Before we do anything else, we need to work out exactly what Mum's job is. She's not some sort of international jet-setting super spy, obviously. She's at home all day! And there's no way she could go out on some sort of mission and be back in time to cook tea! I think she must be a low-level operative. I think she's a sort of monitoring station, tapping into stuff and passing it on to MI5, or whoever."

"I think you should shut up now," said Karen angrily. She headed for the landline in the living room. "We have to get help."

Suddenly, she stopped dead in her tracks. Shock made her let out a half-scream. Sam looked over his shoulder. Silhouetted in the broken back door, at the far end of the kitchen, was the man with the scar. He stood absolutely still. His gun was aimed squarely at them.

"They're here alright," he called.

He took a step forward. The scar across his lips twitched as he smiled.

"Calling the Old Bill?" he said. "I warned you not to."

"I-I-I haven't even picked the phone up yet," stammered Karen.

"Don't muck me about, girl," he said. "You know what I'm talking about."

"We don't!" cried Sam.

Two of the others appeared behind the one with the scar. All three raised their guns.

"Switch it off. Now."

With a sudden lunge, Sam knocked Karen through the doorway into the living room. A dozen shots, muffled by silencers into sharp spits of sound, slapped into the floor where they'd been standing.

"There's too much at stake," yelled the scarred one. "Kill them!"

Sam slammed the living room door shut and heaved the nearby sofa across the doorway. The door buckled under a powerful blow.

"Out the window!" hissed Sam.

Karen fumbled with the handle of the double glazed window which overlooked the street. The living room door split with a loud crunching sound. The barrel of a gun poked through. Three quick shots blew lumps out of the wall opposite.

The window swung open. Sam pushed Karen out, and the pair of them tumbled onto the small lawn at the front of the house.

A pane of glass beside them suddenly shattered. Glass burst outwards across the grass.

"Move!" wailed Sam.

Neither of them dared to look back. They pelted across the road and dived behind the hedges that bordered a neighbour's garden.

They heard the sound of more glass shattering. The gang's fake police car roared into view at the far end of the street.

The only advantage the two of them had was that they knew this area far better than the terrorists. They dodged between houses and over fences. Here and there an angry resident shouted about young hooligans causing trouble. In the distance, they could hear the gang shouting questions to confused neighbours.

✶✶✶✶✶✶

"Time?" said Thirteen.

Thirteen and Two-Twenty-Four were crouched in the back of a speeding van. They rocked in their seats as the vehicle jolted.

Two-Twenty-Four checked his watch.

"9:58am. Six hours until the bomb goes off."

CHAPTER SIX

TRAIN TRACK

"The next train on Platform 2 is the 10:24 service to London Marylebone..."

A nasal voice crept from the speakers above the railway station platform. Sam and Karen sat out of sight, in the metal and Perspex shelter that nestled against the overgrown bushes which bordered Platform 2.

"Why is it always so damp in here?" muttered Sam glumly. "Who's it a shelter for, us or the rain?"

"Have you got the card?" said Karen.

Sam tapped at his shirt pocket and nodded. "Safe and sound."

Their local train station was small, two bare platforms and a ticket kiosk. It was perched half way up a hill, so that travelling in either direction – north towards Birmingham, or south towards London – took you along raised viaducts which gave you a grandly elevated view of the town.

Right now, there was nobody on Platform 1,

on the other side of the rail tracks. Only three other people were waiting at Platform 2: two men carrying briefcases, and a young woman hauling an enormous pink-patterned wheelie suitcase. None of them seemed to be taking any interest in Sam or Karen.

Their hearts still hadn't stopped pounding. They had retreated to the shelter in case one of the terrorists turned up here searching for them. They had no idea that the SD card in Sam's pocket was giving away their precise location to anyone who might want to track them.

Karen kept glancing nervously at the two men carrying briefcases. "Neither has used a phone. They'd have called for back-up if they were with the terrorists, right?"

"S'pose so," mumbled Sam. "I don't think we need worry about any of these three. They'd have done something by now."

He made a conscious effort to breathe slowly. Calm down, he told himself.

He'd never been so scared in his life. This wasn't like the movies. This was *not* like the movies.

Absent-mindedly, he placed a hand against his shirt pocket. At least the data was safe.

A metallic singing hissed through the air. Sam's heart skipped wildly, until he realised it was only the tracks echoing the approaching train. He and Karen stepped out of the shelter as the train slid into view, its wheels clacking a rhythm and its brakes squealing gently.

They headed for the front carriage. It would be closest to the ticket barrier at the other end of the journey, so they could make the quickest getaway. The yellow light blinked on the carriage door and it swung aside with a hydraulic hiss. Half a dozen people got off, Sam and Karen got on. One of the men with briefcases got on behind them.

They didn't look back. If they had, they might have spotted Thirteen and Two-Twenty-Four, hurrying across Platform 2 and hopping onto the train just before the doors hissed shut again.

Sam and Karen walked along the carriage's aisle, between the two rows of stripy blue seats. Discarded newspapers perched here and there. An empty paper coffee cup was jammed into a holder beneath the window. The carriage had a faint smell of dust and feet about it.

Sam looked around. There were one, two... five, six...nine other people in this section. They all seemed to be minding their own business.

Seemed.

None of them looked like terrorists. Stupid!

What was a terrorist supposed to look like, dum-dum? Wearing a balaclava and holding a machine gun?

Sam and Karen took up positions at the far end of the aisle, right up against the driver's cabin, facing back along the carriage. That way, trouble could only approach them from one direction.

Unless a terrorist was driving the train. Unless the real driver was lying slumped on the floor of his cabin, knocked out, while...

Stop it! Sam shut his eyes tightly for a moment. Deep breaths. Stay calm.

"You OK?" whispered Karen.

Sam blinked. "Yeah, yeah. You?"

"Yeah."

Sam could tell she was lying. She was every bit as terrified as he was. She was slightly better at hiding it, that was all.

Sam slumped into his seat. The tea-stained, slightly greasy fabric creaked beneath him. He puffed out his cheeks. Nothing to read. Nothing to do but keep watch.

Looking for what, exactly? As he'd already said to Karen, if those terrorists could look like police officers, they could look like anyone.

The train had moved clear of the station platform. It slowly gathered speed, bumping and ka-klunking softly. Outside, the ground fell away as the train moved across a tall bridge spanning a busy road. Then the roofs of houses and factories came into view, a church tower further off in the distance.

Daylight swept across the carriage in steadily moving beams, like searchlights. One of the beams glanced across a man sitting three rows ahead of Sam, facing him.

It was one of the men from the platform. For a split second, he looked up from the papers he'd taken from his briefcase, and looked directly at Sam.

Sam's brain suddenly lurched. Was this guy watching them? Had they been wrong, was he one of the terrorists after all?

The man was about fifty or so, with greying hair and a small collection of chins. He was shuffling through his papers, tut-tutting here and there. He plucked a pen from his jacket and started scribbling.

No. Maybe not. Just a passenger.

Sam scanned around the carriage. The others were reading paperbacks or newspapers, or just staring sleepily out at the shifting daylight. One person was actually asleep. A tiny electric tapping sound came from the white headphones jammed into his ears.

The train rattled on. One stop, then another. Soon, they were just twenty minutes or so from London.

From where Sam was sitting, he had a clear view all the way down the carriage and, through the glass-panelled connecting doors, into the carriage beyond. The second carriage seemed to give a slight, dizzying tilt, left and right, as the train sped along curved sections of track.

A bored-looking railway employee, wearing a brightly coloured waistcoat, heaved a tall metal trolley into view. He manoeuvred it awkwardly down the aisle and back again.

"Coffees, teas, sandwiches, crisps," he intoned. "Coffees, teas, sandwiches, crisps..."

Nobody wanted any coffee, tea, sandwiches or crisps. With a series of shuddering jolts, he hauled the trolley through into the second carriage. The glass doors cut off the sound of his voice.

As he moved further on, and out of sight, Sam noticed two people squeeze around him and start making their way slowly along the aisle. One was a tall, smartly dressed woman, with very blonde hair and a round face. The other was a man in jeans and a leather jacket. He kept looking at a smartphone gripped in his left hand.

Something about these two set off a small,

quiet alarm in Sam's head. Why? They looked perfectly normal. Why should they strike him as odd?

Was it that they seemed an unlikely couple? They were together – Sam could see them exchange a few whispered words. Was it that they didn't seem to fit together? That they looked too different from each other?

The train rounded another long curve, and the second carriage slid out of sight for a few moments. When its aisle lined up with the first carriage's once more, the two strangers were closer.

Sam watched them carefully. They were definitely coming this way. They were two thirds of the way along the second carriage now.

Why were they making him feel so uneasy? Was it that they weren't sitting down? The train wasn't crowded, there were quite a few spare seats, but these two were looking left and right, and not settling anywhere. Were they just fussy? Or were they looking for something? Or someone?

The train banked along another curve. The second carriage – and the two strangers - glided from view again, this time in the opposite direction. The carriages clunked along. The curve went on for several hundred metres. Lines of trees and undulating wooden fences flowed past.

The train straightened. Those two were almost at the glass doors now. The man kept looking at his smartphone. Sam sat up a little. His nerves were starting to buzz.

The strangers moved past the luggage racks, and the woman pressed the button in the centre of the connecting doors. They hissed aside.

Sam nudged Karen. But he didn't need to, she'd noticed them as well.

✶✶✶✶✶

Thirteen and Two-Twenty-Four knew that they were now closing in on their target, whoever it was, on the run with the SD card. Any of the eleven passengers in this front carriage could be carrying it. No, nine. Those two at the end there were just kids. It obviously couldn't be them.

Two-Twenty-Four kept a sharp eye on the numbers flashing silently across his smartphone. They indicated signal strength and approximate compass bearing. The target was very close.

Thirteen checked out the passengers. Best guess: the sleeping one wasn't asleep at all. No, hardly likely.

None of them looked likely!

Two-Twenty-Four was equally puzzled. He whispered to Thirteen: "Maybe they found the transmitter, ditched the SD card under a seat?"

"No," whispered Thirteen. "If they'd found it, they'd have switched it off. They still want the data."

Two-Twenty-Four watched the numbers on his phone. The card was within metres now!

Sam and Karen sat frozen with fear. Sam felt as if his thoughts were stuck in a loop: *please don't be terrorists, please ignore us, please don't be terrorists, please ignore us...*

The man and the woman were barely three metres away. Closing in. They passed the sleeping guy. They passed the man with the briefcase. There were no other passengers left now.

Two-Twenty-Four turned to Thirteen, then pointed to Sam and Karen. "It's them," he said.

The four of them stared at each other for the space of a heartbeat. Sam and Karen could hardly believe that the terrorists had tracked them down. Thirteen and Two-Twenty-Four could hardly believe that the enemies they'd been chasing were a couple of children.

"You're coming with us," said Thirteen quietly.

CHAPTER SEVEN

ESCAPE

"Go!" yelled Sam.

Sam and Karen sprang to their feet, and were up and over the backs of the seats in front of them before Thirteen and Two-Twenty-Four had time to react. They'd never been so grateful for being

kids before, their size and weight allowing them to scramble out of the adults' way.

Sam grabbed a hefty bag from the overhead shelf and pulled hard. The bag spun out into mid-air behind him, knocking Two-Twenty-Four off balance.

The other passengers in the carriage started complaining loudly. Sam and Karen didn't look to see how close behind them Thirteen and Two-Twenty-Four were. Sam stabbed at the button on the connecting doors and they squashed themselves through as soon as the gap was wide enough. Meanwhile, the sleeping passenger kept on sleeping.

Sam and Karen hurried along the second carriage, weaving in and out of people with quick mutters of "'scuse me" and "Sorry".

"Where are we going?" cried Karen. "We're on a train!"

"Away from those two!" said Sam. "That's all I'm worried about at the moment."

They'd almost got as far as the third carriage, when they heard Thirteen's voice bark out an order behind them: "Wait! You two! Wait!"

"Quick!" squeaked Sam.

They dashed through into the next carriage. Their path was blocked by the bored-looking guy who was lugging the refreshments trolley. Most of the seats were taken in this section. Climbing over them would mean stepping on heads.

"We're caught like rats in a trap!" gasped Karen.

"I've got an idea," said Sam. "I read this in a detective story once."

He squeezed around one side of the trolley. The bored-looking guy was handing a bag of peanuts to a lady on the other side of the aisle. As he pocketed the lady's money, he gawped up at Sam.

"C'n I help you? Coffees, teas, sandwiches, crisps?"

"Yes, please, I'm starving. I'll have this bottle of water, please, and these sandwiches, and these biscuits."

"What are you doing?" gasped Karen. "We're being hunted down, and you're hungry?"

Sam gave her a do-as-I-say look. "I'm sure you're starving too. Here, have some sandwiches, and some more sandwiches, and this can of lemonade."

"Twenty-three ninety," droned the bored-looking guy.

"Brilliant," declared Sam. "We're just kids, so our uncle and auntie are paying for these. They're coming up right behind us. She's very blonde and he's in a leather jacket."

"'K," said the bored-looking guy. He turned away and grasped the trolley's handle.

Sam and Karen scampered as fast as they could into the next carriage. "That should delay them a few minutes at least," said Sam. "Enough time to find a hiding place."

"Like where?" wailed Karen. "What are we going to do, crouch down and pretend to be suitcases?"

"What's the time?"

"Err, 11:35am."

"We'll be at Marylebone in a matter of minutes," said Sam. "If we can just keep out of sight until then. How did they find us?"

"Maybe the guy in the jacket had a photo on his phone? The ones who came to the house must have taken it."

"Yes, I suppose so," said Sam. He wasn't entirely convinced, but no other explanation occurred to him.

The train jolted over a set of points. Karen kept looking back the way they had come, expecting to see Thirteen or Two-Twenty-Four at any second.

Sam led them to the next point at which carriages joined. There were exit doors on each side of the carriage.

"Which side will the platform be?" he said.

Karen tried to remember the last time she'd made this journey, with Mum, visiting her friend Charlotte. "Umm, on the left, I think," she said, screwing up her eyes in concentration.

"OK, in here," said Sam. He opened the door to the toilet that stood next to the left hand exit, and ushered Karen into it.

"Eurgh, it stinks!" moaned Karen.

"You want to stay out here where they can see us?"

She pinched her nose and stepped inside.

They felt the train rattle and slow down. A voice crackled from the ceiling loudspeaker out in the corridor: "Our next station stop is London Marylebone. This train terminates here. Please be sure to take all your belongings with you."

Sam tried to listen for movement outside the toilet door. Karen tried to stand perfectly balanced, so that there was no danger of touching any of the grimy surfaces.

"I think there are people lining up by the door," whispered Sam. "Waiting to get off. As soon as the train stops, we open this door and get out as fast as possible."

"And what if those two are standing right there in the queue?" whispered Karen.

Sam considered for a moment. "Don't know.

We'll have to risk it. But I don't think they'll, y'know...shoot us. Not in a crowded place."

"You really think so?"

"No, not really."

There was a loud banging on the toilet door. They both flinched. "Oi! How long you gonna be in there?"

Neither of them dared answer. Beneath their feet, they felt the train slow down further. Its wheels clattered in a steady one-two-three.

"Oi!"

They heard whoever-it-was clump away, grumbling. The train squealed to a stop. They rocked unsteadily.

"Ready?" whispered Sam.

"No," whispered Karen.

They waited until they heard the exit doors swoosh aside. Then Sam quickly opened the toilet door and they leapt out. There was a large knot of people jostling around the exit.

None of them were Thirteen or Two-Twenty-Four. All of them turned to look at Sam and Karen with disgust as the air from inside the toilet rolled over them.

Sam nudged his way into the tightly packed passengers. "Sorry, she's quite ill! I think she's going to throw up now!"

With a collective gasp, the passengers parted to let them through. Karen, scarlet with embarrassment, pushed Sam out of the train and onto the platform. The air suddenly felt cool in their lungs, and had the distinctive scent of London about it.

"You pig!" she hissed at her brother.

"Got us out, didn't it?"

"We've got to lose ourselves in the crowd," said Karen. "And quickly - those two will be out here any minute."

Being shorter than most of the other passengers was a factor in their favour. They sped along the platform, keeping close to wherever the shifting bustle of travellers was thickest. They followed a madly wandering path, dodging from one group of passengers to another, trying to look as if they were attached to this set of adults, then that, then another.

Thirteen and Two-Twenty-Four battled their way out of the train. As they stepped onto the platform, they were met by a uniformed officer with "British Transport Police" printed on his reflective jacket.

"Can I have a word, please, sir, madam?" he said sternly. "This train called ahead and said you'd refused to pay for sundry goods and - "

Thirteen grunted angrily, reached into her suit and flashed an ID at him. "We're with the security services, get out of the way."

"MI5?" grinned the uniformed officer. "Oh, brilliant! I've always wanted to - "

"Shut up," said Thirteen. She turned to a man wearing a chunky anorak, who'd just appeared out of the crowd. This was another MI5 agent, numbered Four-Eleven. He was out of breath.

"Well?" snapped Thirteen.

"Sorry, ma'am," gasped Four-Eleven. "Lost them. The tracker's getting scrambled signals in here, too many people have got their phones on."

Thirteen swore under her breath. "Spread out. They won't be far away. Send some men into the Underground, the rest at street level."

Four-Eleven nodded, turned and hurried away.

"Those idiot kids!" hissed Thirteen. "Do they have any idea what danger they're in?"

By now, the uniformed officer was fed up of being left out. "What's going on here?" he demanded. "Who are you after?"

Thirteen sighed. "You might as well know. At this rate, we're going to need every officer in London! One of our low-level surveillance agents picked up details of a terrorist plot last night. This morning, she was kidnapped. The terrorists think they got to her before she could tell us their plans – which was what we wanted them to think. So we've got a perfect opportunity to catch an entire terrorist cell red-handed, planting a bomb, this afternoon. If nothing goes wrong."

"What about your kidnapped agent?" asked the uniformed officer.

"We know where she is, she'll be safe soon," said Thirteen dismissively.

"So, if you're after terrorists - why are you chasing a couple of kids?"

Thirteen gritted her teeth. "They're what might go wrong. Months of undercover work have gone into this operation. Those two could ruin everything. And get themselves killed into the bargain!"

CHAPTER EIGHT

PINK BIKE

Karen's friend Charlotte lived quite close to the railway station. They'd been best friends during the first years of primary school, and when Charlotte's family moved down to London they'd kept in touch.

"We'd better not tell her the truth," said Sam.

They clattered up the stone steps that led to Charlotte's front door.

"Why?" said Karen. "We can trust Charlotte."

"Yes, but can we trust her to keep quiet once we're gone?"

Karen rat-tat-tatted the knocker and Charlotte's mum appeared a few seconds later. She was wiping flour off her fingers with a tea towel.

"Hello Karen!" she said with a smile. "Sam! What a lovely surprise! We weren't supposed to be expecting you, were we?"

"No, we've just dropped by," said Karen. Sam jabbed her in the ribs. "To ask a favour," she added.

Charlotte's mum twisted around to shout up the stairs. "Charlotte! Karen's here!" She turned back to them. "Come on in."

Sam nudged Karen again. "We can't stop," said Karen. "Sorry, we're..." She turned to Sam. "What was it?"

Sam felt like screaming. "We're doing a thing for school. Geography project," he said calmly to Charlotte's mum. "It's timed, and we've only got the next few hours. Can we borrow two bikes?"

Charlotte's mum glanced up and down the street. "Is your mum not here?"

"She's, umm..." said Karen.

"She's at the finish line," piped up Sam. "In the city centre. Navigating around is part of it, it's, er, a sort of initiative test."

"Oh," said Charlotte's mum, not entirely convinced. "Charlotte! Karen's here!... Are you listening? Charlotte!" She turned back to Sam and Karen, brushing flour off her sleeves. "Look, are you sure? Wouldn't you be better taking the tube? The traffic can be very dangerous."

"We, umm, er..." said Sam.

"Oh, a lot of it is off-road!" said Karen suddenly. "No traffic."

Charlotte came rumbling down the stairs, and once the two girls had exchanged hugs, Sam and

Karen found themselves having to go through the whole fake story thing again.

Sam kept glancing at Karen's watch.

12:09pm.

"Sure," said Charlotte, "you can borrow my bike and Mum's. That's OK, isn't it, Mum?"

Another ten minutes went by before Sam and Karen were at the side of the road with both bicycles. Then another three minutes went by as the pair of them argued about who was going to ride which bike. Charlotte's mum's bike was too big for Sam, and Charlotte's was too girly.

"I'm not riding around on that!" cried Sam. "It's pink!"

"This was your idea!" said Karen.

"Not to ride around on a bike that's pink, it wasn't!"

"Then let's use the Underground!" said Karen.

"No, we need to keep out of sight."

"Then ride the pink bike."

They set off, keeping to the broad pavement on the other side of the street. Karen had visited Charlotte enough over the past couple of years to have a good idea of which direction they needed to go in.

12:31pm. Three and a half hours until the bomb went off.

CHAPTER NINE

CAR CHASE

They pedalled through a series of side roads, keeping away from crowded areas as much as possible. They blended into the background noise and movement of the city, picking their way through a criss-cross of cars and people, and more people and more cars, honking vans and sour-faced shoppers. Glass and concrete rose up high around them, funnelling them through its valleys, whisking air into their faces which was heavy with the scent of vehicles and cooking. Sam was very confident that nobody, nobody at all, would be able to track them down in the middle of all this urban chaos.

"That big car coming towards us, the BMW," said Karen, slowing down slightly to pull level with Sam. "I saw it three streets back."

"It's just going the same way as us, that's all," said Sam.

"Don't be stupid, it's coming this way," said

Karen. "It must have double backed to get up ahead like that. I think it's following us."

Sam hoped she was wrong. He hoped she was wrong more than he'd ever hoped for anything. The BMW was about a hundred metres away, gliding steadily ahead.

It slowed at a zebra crossing. Coming up on Sam and Karen's left was a wide turning marked with a "No Through Road" sign. As they drew level with it, Sam whistled sharply at his sister.

"Down here! It's a dead end, we'll soon see if they're following us!"

"D'err! Dead end? If they're after us, we'll be trapped!" cried Karen.

Sam pointed to the far end of the cul-de-sac. What made the street a dead end for cars was a large set of raised flowerbeds, surrounded by pavements and concrete bollards. Their bikes could simply swerve around it all and come out on the road beyond.

Quickly, they turned left and made for the flowerbeds. Sam looked over his shoulder. His stomach did a somersault as he saw the BMW turn the same corner behind them.

"Always got to be right, haven't you," he muttered under his breath. "Move!" he called to Karen.

She shot a glance over her shoulder too. Both of them pedalled harder.

The BMW speeded up. Sam could hear the growling throb of its engine, like a stalking tiger nearing its prey.

"Must be the two on the train!" he shouted to Karen. "Faster!"

Sam lifted off the seat of his bike as he shifted all his weight onto the pedals. The bike's tyres swished a rapid beat against the road's surface, but the sound was gradually drowned out by the roaring of the car behind.

The bikes careered ahead, swooping up onto the pavement by bumping across a flattened section in front of a driveway. Sam and Karen shot along the wide tarmac beside the raised flowerbeds.

"Ha! That'll stop 'em!" yelled Sam in triumph.

They both braked sharply as they emerged beside a busy road overlooking a large park. Sam's back wheel skidded in a semi-circle.

The grin on his face suddenly vanished as he watched the BMW swerve and bump up on the pavement. Without slowing for a moment, it lined up with the paved area beside the flowerbeds and roared on. Sunlight flashed across its windscreen.

Sam let out a couple of words which would have got him into trouble on any other day. He jumped back onto the bike, his legs feeling like wet spaghetti.

"Get out of its way!" screamed Karen.

The car rocketed past the flowerbeds, its snarl echoing loudly off the brickwork around it. With a yelp of terror, Sam pedalled out of its path. The car's front bumper missed his back wheel by millimetres.

The car burst across the pavement and out onto the main road. There was a screaming of brakes as several other cars twisted to avoid it. Horns blared angrily. The BMW left smoking tyre marks as it turned a sharp ninety degrees.

Sam and Karen scrambled to get the bikes back up to full speed, hearts thumping. The muscles in Sam's legs were beginning to feel like jelly.

"Park gates! Over there!" yelled Karen.

The leafy park on the opposite side of the road was ringed by a high metal fence. About a hundred metres further up the street was a broad opening where a grey tarmac path led off across the grass.

Sam and Karen headed straight for it, but they were still on the wrong side of the road. They would have to cross in front of the BMW. They sped on, weaving past a couple of pedestrians.

The BMW revved up behind them. It shot forward twenty metres, then found its way blocked by a Mini which had jack-knifed to avoid hitting the confusion of vehicles which the chase had caused. It had stalled, the driver caught between fury at the BMW's reckless driving and fright at the imminent danger.

With the Mini standing still, its horn screeching, the BMW roared around it, rocking violently as it bounced up the kerb. The delay was enough for Sam and Karen to zip across the road. The traffic had all stopped in its tracks.

The bikes whipped along the tarmac and dived into the park. Sam's entire body seemed to have turned into jelly now. Every breath felt like sand in his lungs.

The BMW, gaining speed once more, bashed the corner of a van out of its way. Without slowing for a moment, it lurched up onto the tarmac path, leaving the van teetering at the side of the road, with steam gushing from under its hood and the remains of a headlight scattered everywhere.

Sam looked back, and wished he hadn't. His eyes kept wanting to shut tight, and discover that today was only a terrible nightmare, but the black BMW ninety metres behind them was all too real. Sam's legs ached. His feet kicked at the pedals. The two bikes scurried on, like panicking mice fleeing from a cobra.

Ahead, the tarmac path led down to a lake. They'd have to go another way. Without exchanging a word, they both realised that the only option was to cut across the huge open lawn to their right.

The grass was short, recently cut. Even so, there was no way the bikes could maintain the same speed as they'd managed on the path. They pedalled as hard as they could. The ground beneath them rumbled and bumped. The BMW barely slowed down at all.

Panic stopped Sam from seeing the stony patch ahead. His front wheel scraped sharply. He was aware of being thrown over the handlebars. Then the grass seemed to leap up and smack him hard in the chest. He rolled, the bike bouncing into a heap beside him.

"Sam!" screamed Karen.

He had no idea how he'd managed to get to his feet, but he was up and reaching for the bike. The pursuing car veered slightly to one side. The window by the front passenger seat slid open and a face appeared.

Sam's heart tightened. The face was that of the scarred terrorist, the one from this morning's raid. His arm emerged, gripping a dark, stubby pistol.

Three rapid shots sent tufts of grass and earth leaping from the ground around Sam. Then the boy was back on his bike, with his feet pedalling and his brain registering with relief that its wheels hadn't buckled in the crash.

The BMW turned a full circle, grinding up the grass into mud. It accelerated, heading straight for them once more.

"They're not giving up," cried Karen, close to tears. "They're going to kill us."

The two bikes sped on. The grass began to

slope downwards. The BMW was gaining on them every second.

Sam looked around, desperately scanning the landscape for something that might allow them to escape. The grass continued on down a shallow hill. Beyond that was another path, this one dotted with people, beside a small playground and a crazy golf course.

The bikes speeded up slightly, hurtling down the sloping grass, their wheels rattling and shaking all the way. Sam's fingers gripped the handlebars so tightly he felt his palms sweating.

They had to decide. Which way? On open ground, the car could easily catch up. It was barely twenty metres behind them now.

Two more shots rang out. One of them smacked into the ground close to Sam's front wheel.

Karen glanced back. The man with the scar was leaning out of the passenger window. His arm was extended, the pistol held up so that he could aim more accurately. Only the rapid shuddering of the vehicle over the grass was stopping him getting a clear shot.

They were nearing the next tarmac path. They couldn't take it, there were too many people, but where it snaked away behind the hill they were descending, there was a short underpass. A dark rectangle vanished into the earth, like an orderly cave mouth.

"How wide d'you think that underpass is?" shouted Karen.

"What? Dunno," shouted Sam. "Not very."

He saw what she was getting at. Going into the underpass was going to be a big risk, but right now there seemed to be no alternative. They headed straight for it.

The man with the scar fired three more shots. One of them chipped the frame beneath Sam's saddle. The whole bike shook, but with a howling yell of effort Sam kept it balanced.

Nearly at the underpass. Thirty metres, twenty-five, twenty. The BMW's driver shouted to the one with the scar. He dropped back inside the car.

Ten metres, five, four, three. The two bikes shot into the darkness of the underpass. Echoes scattered around the white tiled walls. Sam and Karen flinched as the sound of the BMW's engine was added to the deafening reverberations in the tunnel.

Suddenly, there was a glittering explosion of sparks in the darkness. Sam and Karen's gamble was paying off: the tunnel was only a fraction wider than the BMW.

The passenger side of the car hit the tiles at full speed. The wing mirror exploded into fragments. Both doors buckled, sending sparks in all directions as the metal was scraped bare. The impact bounced the BMW sideways and the driver's side smashed against the opposite wall.

The echoes in the tunnel made Sam's ears throb. The BMW's front bumper suddenly crumpled. The driver battled with the steering wheel. The one with the scar cowered behind the dashboard. The car ricocheted from one side of the tunnel to the other, and with a screaming crash of metal and a rupturing of tyres, it scraped to a halt.

Sam and Karen could hear the occupants of the car shouting angrily at each other. The bikes shot out of the other end of the underpass, into bright daylight.

They didn't stop pedalling until they reached the far end of the park, and the next main road.

✳✳✳✳✳

Sam's lungs felt as if they'd been microwaved. "That..." he gasped breathlessly, "was very... close."

Karen was propped against her bike, her feet tightly together on the pavement in an effort to stop them shaking. She held her face in her hands, letting out a sharp breath here and there, and the occasional exclamation of relief.

It was 1:25pm

"How long do you think we've got?" said Sam. "Until they're on our trail again?"

"I don't know," said Karen. "Probably not long."

She thought about Mum. Where was she at this moment? Was she OK? Karen gripped her teeth together, to stop her jaw shuddering with emotion.

70

Sam leaned over and inspected the bullet-chipped frame of his bike. "Not bad, considering it's pink," he muttered.

He felt something grate in his shirt pocket. With a rush of alarm, he reached for the SD card. He pulled out a handful of plastic splinters. It had smashed when he fell.

*****

Several miles away, Two-Twenty-Four gave Thirteen the bad news. "The transmitter's gone dark, ma'am."

Thirteen tapped her fingers rapidly against her side. Had they found it, and turned it off? Had someone else? Had they been captured? Were they dead already?

"We have no way of tracking them at all," said Two-Twenty-Four. "I've got our people tapping into CCTV cameras on the streets, but it might take hours to find them."

Thirteen checked the time. 1:33pm. "Then they're completely on their own," she said.

CHAPTER TEN

WESTMINSTER BRIDGE

"Oh, that's great!" cried Karen, with every scrap of sarcasm she could muster. "That's just great! The card is broken. Fan-blasted-tastic! Well, doesn't that just put the cherry on top of this wonderful, wonderful day!"

"Yeah, OK," muttered Sam.

"We now have no proof," said Karen. "We have no proof of this terrorist plot. None. It was all on that card, and that card is broken. I say we go to the nearest police station. Now! We are in over our heads."

"We still have no idea who to trust!" protested Sam.

"Er, hello, knock knock, did you not realise we were almost killed back there?"

"And an awful lot of other people are going to get killed if we don't do something about those terrorists," said Sam.

"And how exactly is that going to benefit

Mum?" yelled Karen. "You think it's all just going to work out fine, like in a book or a movie? Do you?"

Sam simply glared at her. He didn't want to admit even to himself, let alone to Karen, that yes, that's exactly what he'd thought. However, today was teaching him something rather different.

They sat at the side of the road in silence for several minutes. Traffic snarled and tooted past them. At last, they clambered back on their bikes and headed once more in the direction of the Thames.

The city seemed even more hostile now, even more alive with shadows and dangers. Anyone they happened to pass might be an enemy. Anyone who even noticed them might be part of a surveillance team.

Sam kept his eyes down as much as possible, letting Karen lead the way. He watched the patchwork of pavements moving past beneath him, his hands on the handlebars, his feet steadily pushing the pedals.

Several times, he fought back a rush of fear which threatened to overwhelm him. He tried not to think about how alone they were, how vulnerable and how foolhardy. He tried to concentrate on the terrorists' plot, on the bomb that would be planted soon, on why they were here in the first place.

They kept to smaller roads and pathways as much as possible. Whenever their route allowed them to cut across a pedestrian-only area, they took it to keep out of sight of any vehicles which might be following them. The fact that the SD card was smashed meant that nobody, terrorists or MI5, knew their location, but not knowing that kept them wary and terrified.

3:22pm. They emerged from a side street onto the noisy, multi-laned chaos of the Thames embankment. Ahead of them, across the road, past a line of tall trees, was the river. And to their right, a short way upstream, was Westminster Bridge.

"There it is," said Sam. "That's where they're planting the bomb. And it could be any time now, if they're planning to set it off at four o'clock."

They made for the nearest road crossing. Sam's heart thumped faster with every passing minute.

"We've got to be very careful here," said Karen. "We have no idea what to expect. They might be watching out for us."

"I'd be amazed if they weren't," said Sam.

"They might think they've scared us off?" said Karen hopefully. "Trying to run us down like that?"

They looked at each other. "Nah," they both said.

Approaching the bridge was easier than they expected. There was a high concrete wall which ran alongside the pavement, and which kept them out of sight of anyone on the bridge itself. As the wall finally dipped away, they got their first proper look at where they were heading.

The Thames glittered in the daylight. Its surface chopped and bobbed, and its tea-brown murkiness swirled in the wake of a dozen or more small vessels that chugged along it. Westminster Bridge stood broad and solid, a steady stream of cars and buses shuffling across it.

Broad and solid for how long? wondered Sam. What might it look like, if he and Karen failed in their mission?

Beside the river loomed the massive shape of the Houses of Parliament, the clock tower of Big Ben rising up above the gothic, spiky architecture of the main buildings.

"It's bigger than it looks on telly," mumbled Sam.

Karen propped her bike against a set of railings. She scanned the area, shielding her eyes with her hand. "What now?" she said. "Where do we look? What do we look for?"

3:31pm.   Twenty-nine minutes until detonation.

Slowly, looking around them for the slightest clue, they walked onto the bridge. Traffic honked along. People walked at speed, back and forth, ignoring these two kids who seemed to be slightly lost.

Sam and Karen gradually crossed the river. Sam felt as if his nervous system was about to tear itself apart like a paper tissue in a washing machine.

3:40pm. Twenty minutes until detonation.

"Anything?" said Karen.

"No," said Sam. "Something's got to happen soon."

They made their way back again. More traffic, more people, more time passing, more absolutely nothing.

3:50pm. Ten minutes until detonation.

A large, dark blue car, a people carrier, glided into view. It was moving slower than the other cars. An impatient taxi honked its way around it. Sam nudged Karen sharply.

"See it?"

"Yes."

"We've got to get closer," said Sam. "See who's inside. My guess is it's the guy with the scar. Keep walking, blend in with everyone else."

The car slowly approached. They closed in on it, matching their speed to the other pedestrians.

Sam could see three figures in the car. Reflections off the windscreen kept the ones sitting up front hidden, but the person behind them was becoming more distinct. Within seconds, he could see that it was:

"Mum!"

Luckily, his cry wasn't loud enough to have been overheard in the people carrier. Karen gripped his arm.

"She's safe!"

"Or she will be once we get her away from there," said Sam. Conflicting thoughts raced through his head. What was the best course of action? What could they do?

As the people carrier slowed to a stop, the two sitting up front came into view. They were Thirteen and Two-Twenty-Four. Both were looking straight ahead; neither of them had spotted Sam or Karen.

"The terrorists!" hissed Sam, making the same mistake they'd made on the train. "They must have the bomb with them right now. It must be the car!"

Mum had to be rescued, and the terrorists had to be sent packing.

A plan suddenly popped into his head. Quickly, he stepped forward and flung open the back door of the people carrier. Mum's gaze whipped around at him and she gasped.

"Sam! What the-?"

"Mum! Get out!" he yelled. He grabbed her sleeve and hauled at her as hard as he could. She half-jumped, half-fell out of the car. Instantly, Thirteen and Two-Twenty-Four leaped from their seats.

Sam turned and shouted at the top of his voice, to passers-by, to the traffic, to anyone and everyone:

"Help! Police! Call the cops! These people have a bomb! Get away from here, all of you! There's a bomb in this car! Call the cops!"

People stopped and stared. Others took a step back, wondering what this kid was playing at. One or two looked from Sam to the car and back again and pulled out their phones.

For a second, Sam felt on top of the world. Mum was all but safe, and there was no way now that these terrorists could plant a bomb here, not with everyone watching like this.

"Sam!" cried Mum angrily. "What are you doing?"

"Saving your life, what does it look like?" cried Sam. Talk about ungrateful!

Mum grabbed him by the shoulders. "These people are from MI5!" she hissed. "I was rescued half an hour ago."

Suddenly, Sam felt as if his insides had shrivelled up to the size of a pea. Two-Twenty-Four hurried over to the people who were phoning the cops, flashing an ID badge and trying to contain the situation.

"Oh no," wailed Karen. "These two weren't out to get us on the train, they were trying to help us!"

"Sam, what have you done?" said Mum.

Thirteen looked like she might burst with anger. "Get in that car! Out of sight! Now!" She added a few words that Sam normally pretended he didn't know.

Then he almost added a few of his own, as he turned to look across the bridge. Karen followed his line of sight.

Visible amongst the criss-cross of people approaching from the far side of the river was the man with the scar. He and Sam saw each other at precisely the same moment. The man was carrying a large reinforced silver case, the sort normally used for cameras or other delicate equipment. That, Sam now realised, was the bomb.

The man had been walking quickly, but now he slowed down. It took a fraction of a second for him to see the MI5 car and realise he'd been walking into a trap. Without hesitation he turned on his heels and hurried back the way he had come.

Neither Thirteen nor Two-Twenty-Four had seen him. They were hurriedly trying to assure the passers-by that nothing was happening. Mum was busy telling her children off for putting themselves in danger. She hadn't spotted the terrorist either.

Sam watched the man walking back into the crowd.

MI5's entire operation was ruined. The man with the scar, and those he was working with, were about to get away.

CHAPTER ELEVEN

HAND TO HAND

Sam was unable to hold anything in his head except the words "all my fault". Almost without thinking, certainly without considering the consequences, he suddenly hurried after the scarred man. He ignored Karen's yell of "Wait!" and Mum's yell of, "Sam! Where are you going?"

"Leave him," said Thirteen grumpily. "He's letting off steam, embarrassed at all the trouble you two kids have caused."

Karen felt a flush of anger. She pulled herself up to her full height and spun Thirteen around to face her. "He is chasing the man with the bomb!" she cried. "On his own!"

Halfway back across the bridge now, the scarred man was half-running, speeding up. Without pausing, he unclipped the catches on the case he was carrying and flipped a switch inside it. Turning off the bomb's timer, thought Sam.

The man wasn't looking back. Here and there he bumped shoulders with someone walking the other way, barging them aside. Sam was rapidly catching him up, staying out of sight in the blur of people, hurrying as fast as those wet spaghetti legs of his would go.

Back at the car, Thirteen and Two-Twenty-Four were craning their necks to spot the man. All they could see was a shifting pattern of heads.

"Do you have a positive ID?" said Thirteen.

"No, ma'am," said Two-Twenty-Four.

Karen felt like screaming. "He's getting away! Sam saw him, I saw him! Do something!"

Thirteen turned to her angrily. "Let's leave the grown-ups in charge here, shall we? We do this by the book. We make an ID!"

For Karen, this was the last straw. She glared up at Thirteen. "My brother and I have been chased, and shot at, and threatened all day! We know those terrorists when we see them, believe me! If you want an ID, you've got one from me! Now *move*!"

Thirteen glared back at her. For a split second, there was a silence between them. Then Thirteen nodded to Two-Twenty-Four.

Two-Twenty-Four quickly speed-dialled and barked orders calling for reinforcements to cut off access to the bridge. Moments later, three large cars identical to Thirteen's people carrier dashed into view on the other side of the river, their tyres howling. They sped across the road, cutting off the traffic. Horns blared. MI5 agents poured out of the cars.

The man with the scar didn't seem worried in the slightest. He continued running, straight ahead. Sam thought he might be about to simply hurl the bomb at the agents, but as he drew level with the bridge's last lamp-post, he darted to one side and out of sight.

He was scurrying down a long, narrow flight of stone steps, heading for a small wharf beside the river bank. Sam arrived at the top of the steps to see a large motorboat rocking gently at the end of the wharf. Another man was in the boat, crouched over the controls. The one with the scar shouted to him, and he fired up the engine. A spray of smoke and water ballooned from the boat's rear.

Sam was half way down the steps. The MI5 agents appeared at the top, yelling at him to get out of the way. He ignored them.

The man with the scar, intent on his escape, paid no attention to them either. As the speedboat revved up, he jumped off the end of the wooden wharf and onto a wide seat near the back of the boat. The silver case containing the bomb was tucked under his arm.

The speedboat roared into motion. Sam was still pelting down the stone steps. The boat swerved and shot forward.

They were getting away! Sam felt a surge of panic. The speedboat moved off quickly, its surging movement taking it past the stone steps. Without hesitation, Sam leapt into mid-air as the boat approached. Behind him came more yells.

Sam hit the small, flat section at the rear of the speedboat with a painful thud. The roar of the boat's engine covered up the thumping sound he made as he landed, and the boat's rocking motion concealed the slight shift he caused to its balance. The two terrorists, intent on what was ahead, hadn't spotted him yet.

The speedboat accelerated. It passed under Westminster Bridge, and Sam was blasted by the echoing drone of the engine.

His grip slipped. One leg suddenly dangled over the water. Spray hissed across his foot. With a yelp of fright, he pulled himself up into a ball.

The man with the scar reached into a locker and pulled out a hefty revolver. He spun around, intending to aim at any agents on the bridge behind him who might also be armed.

Then he saw Sam. His face flashed alarm for a split second, then anger. The MI5 agents standing on the bridge watched helplessly, unable to fire at the boat for fear of hitting Sam.

The scarred man swung his gun around and aimed squarely at Sam. "A hostage!" he cried in triumph. "Better than I'd hoped."

The boat bumped and bucked across the surface of the Thames. Sam took hold of the boat's rear seat and pretended to move into a sitting position.

He kicked out suddenly. The toe of his trainer cracked into the scarred man's knee. The man crumpled, emitting a sharp howl of pain.

The gun went off. Wooden splinters exploded off the boat's back seat. The other terrorist, the boat's driver, screamed at the man with the scar to be careful and get the kid under control, he had to steer this blasted tub! There'd be choppers in the air soon!

Sam leapt at the man with the scar. In his favourite movies, there'd be a scuffle, a fight for the gun. This wasn't a movie. Sam knew he'd never match this man's strength. He knew the terrorist could simply knock him aside, and would shoot him dead. So Sam poked him in the eye, hard.

"Ow! You little – "

Sam kicked at the man's arm. The gun spun

out of his hand and was lost in the foaming spray behind the rocketing speedboat.

The scarred man hit Sam across the chest. He collapsed backwards, winded. The man picked up the silver case containing the bomb, and hurled it at Sam with a bellow of rage. Sam ducked. The case crashed into the rear seat and bounced open.

Embedded inside the case was a small grey-and-green digital timer. It was counting down from one minute. 0:59. 0:58.

Sam's heart skipped a beat. Had the impact reset the bomb's timer?

Before Sam could even think another thought, the man with the scar had seized him by his shoulders and dragged him to one side of the speedboat. Clearly, he'd changed his mind about keeping a hostage. He was going to throw Sam overboard.

Their weight made the boat lean to one side. The driver yelled at the scarred man again, but he wasn't listening. All his attention was focused on getting rid of this kid. He lifted Sam off his feet. Sam's legs kicked and dangled helplessly.

0:44. 0:43. 0:42.

Sam could feel the cold spray of the water leaping up behind him. The tilt of the boat meant he was completely off-balance, at the mercy of the scarred man. For a moment, the terrorist's pale face glared hugely into his own.

As the man heaved Sam up, ready to throw him over the side of the boat, Sam floundered wildly. With his arm at full stretch, his hand caught hold of the boat's large, padded steering wheel.

The driver gave a yell, but before he could smack at Sam's fingers to dislodge them, Sam's pull on the wheel forced the whole speedboat to veer sharply to one side.

Engine screaming, the boat tilted over. Sam was crushed against the side by the scarred man. The driver, trying desperately to keep hold of the steering wheel, lost his footing and flipped over into the thundering river with a screech of fright.

0:26. 0:25. 0:24.

The man with the scar threw himself backwards to avoid tumbling into the water too. The boat regained some balance but Sam, now free from the man's grip, put all his weight into holding the steering wheel at full turn.

The speedboat roared in a wide circle, churning the murky water into a fury. Stop the boat, then stop the bomb, thought Sam. The silver case rattled and bounced around his feet. The little display blinked up at him.

0:19. 0:18. 0:17.

The scarred man staggered and pulled himself upright, both arms holding tightly onto the opposite side of the boat. The steep angle at which the boat was circling was all that was stopping him from launching himself at Sam again. Sam wedged himself behind the wheel. Flecks of icy water splattered the back of his head.

0:13. 0:12. 0:11.

The scarred man dragged himself level with Sam. He reached into his pocket. The knife he pulled out was short, with a vicious serrated edge. He raised it, never taking his eyes off Sam. He prepared to leap at the boy. Sam gripped the steering wheel to stop himself shaking.

The man jumped.

His feet had barely left the deck when Two-Twenty-Four, launching himself from the police patrol boat which had sped up alongside, knocked the scarred man sideways. The man's head bounced off the boat's dashboard and he slumped into unconsciousness. Two-Twenty-Four scrambled to keep his balance on the tilting deck.

"The bomb!" shouted Sam, pointing madly at the silver case. 0:06. 0:05.

Two-Twenty-Four quickly reached over and switched off the timer.

0:04. Click.

Then the MI5 man shuffled across the deck and cut the power to the speedboat's engine. It shuddered to a halt, floating unsteadily and silently on the choppy waters. The police patrol vessel bobbed beside it, packed from stem to stern with MI5 agents and police officers.

Two-Twenty-Four grinned over at Sam. "You going to let go of that steering wheel now?"

CHAPTER TWELVE

BACK TO SCHOOL

"Got everything?" said Mum.

Sam did a quick check. His school bag was fully loaded.

It was the following Monday morning, back to school time. Mum was in a particularly good mood, because Karen was ready to go, and hadn't had to be called twelve times, then told to get dressed twice, then argued with about the importance of a proper breakfast.

"I've even combed my hair," said Karen. "I've decided I'm going to stop wasting time and get things done."

Mum did a comical 'OMG' face. "Wonders will never cease."

"And while we're at school," said Sam to Mum, "don't go causing any major security alerts, OK?"

"Promise," said Mum. "In any case, all the new equipment MI5 have installed in my office makes me practically invisible."

Sam smiled and nodded, and he and his sister left for school. The living room window was still boarded up, but the back door had been replaced.

Sam and Karen were under strict instructions not to say a word about what had happened to anyone at school. The rest of the terrorist cell had been rounded up, and Sam and Karen's part in the entire affair was being officially 'forgotten'. MI5 were getting the credit for a successful anti-terrorist operation, and Sam would never be able to boast about what he'd done.

But, somehow, he didn't want to anyway. Today, the walk to school seemed strangely fresh and new. All those worries he'd had, about leaving Year 6 and starting a new school later in the year, didn't seem anything like as bad now. Year 6 was cool, moving up to Karen's school next autumn was cool, everything was cool.

Funny how things get back to normal, he thought to himself.

Sam Hay

"We'd inherited a business. Maybe we were millionaires!"

Albert Grub has an ordinary life until his dad inherits the famous Piddler's Porridge factory. But the town's noodle tycoon is keen to get his hands on the place. Is he after the legendary Spoon of Doom, supposed to be hidden in the factory? And what can Albert do to stop him?

Jean Ure

"I was caught in a transporter beam!"

Jake is delighted when he's abducted by aliens. Better still,

they want him to carry out an important mission.

The world is in danger, and he can help save it!

The only problem is, the aliens have taken his annoying

sister Rosie too – and she doesn't believe in aliens...

Black Cats
Books to pounce on